GIANT TALES

retold by
Corinne Denan

illustrated by
Bert Dodson

Troll Associates

CONTENTS

Three Golden Hairs

There once was a poor woman whose son was born with the mark of luck upon him. And so they called him a luck-child. It was said that in his seventeenth year he would marry the King's daughter.

Now it so happened that the King himself entered the village a few days after the birth of the luck-child. But no one knew he was the King, because he often wore disguises. In this way, he could find out what his people really thought of him.

"What news is there to tell?" he asked the villagers.

"A few days ago a luck-child was born," they told him. "And it is said that in his seventeenth year, he will marry the King's daughter."

Now the King was a rather disagreeable and evil man. His only daughter was but a few days old herself, and so he was quite disturbed at the thought of a humble villager marrying his beloved child.

Still in disguise, the King went to the home of the luck-child. "You are poor," he said to the parents. "I will take your child and care for him, for I am rich. And I will give you much gold in return."

At first the mother did not wish to give up her child. But her husband persuaded her that the boy would have a good home. And since he was a luck-child anyway, all would go well. Besides, they could certainly use the gold.

So the child was turned over to the King, who put him in a box and rode away. As soon as the wicked King came to a large, deep lake, he tossed the box into the water.

"And that's the end of the unwanted bride-groom," said the King. "I have freed my beloved daughter."

But, as luck would have it, the box did not sink. After the King rode off, the box floated along like a boat. It floated right down to a mill not far from the King's own palace.

The miller's young servant happened to be standing at the water's edge. He drew the box ashore with a long hook, thinking he had found a great treasure. Imagine his surprise when he opened the box and found a smiling baby boy!

The servant took the child to the miller. The miller and his wife had no children of their own.

So they rejoiced in their good luck, and adopted the child. They took good care of him, and he grew into a fine and sturdy lad.

One day when the boy was seventeen years old, a terrible storm arose. The King happened to be riding by the mill at that time. Seeking shelter, the King entered the miller's house. "Is that tall child your son?" the King asked.

"He is my adopted son, but he is like my own," the miller said. "Seventeen years ago I found him in a box that floated down the river."

The evil King knew right away that this was the luck-child he had tried to drown. But he said, "Would you good people ask your son to carry a letter to my wife, the Queen, at the castle? I will reward him with two pieces of gold."

"As the King commands," said the miller.

The King wrote a letter to the Queen. It said: "As soon as this young man arrives with this letter, have him killed and buried. Do this before I return."

So the luck-child set out on the journey to the Queen. But when it grew dark, he lost his way in the forest. Then he saw a small cottage with a light shining from the window. An old woman sat by the fire.

"What do you want?" she asked.

"I come from the mill," said the young man. "I am on my way to deliver a letter to the Queen. But I have lost my way in the forest, and I ask to spend the night here."

"You have made a poor choice," said the woman. "This cottage belongs to robbers. They will surely murder you as soon as they come home."

"I am not afraid," said the young man. "And I can go no farther." So he stretched himself out in front of the fire and fell asleep.

Soon the robbers returned and asked why the young man was there.

"He lost his way," said the old woman. "I took pity on him. He has a letter for the Queen."

The robbers took the letter the King had written, opened it, and read it. They had never liked the evil King so they decided to help the luckchild.

The captain of the robbers ripped up the letter and wrote another. It said: "When this young man arrives, marry him to the Princess immediately. Do this before I return."

The next morning the robbers woke the young man and showed him the way to the castle.

When the Queen read the letter, she was surprised. But she did as the letter said. A splendid marriage feast was prepared, and the King's

daughter and the luck-child were married the very next day.

When the King returned to the palace, he was astonished and angry to discover that the young man had married his daughter after all.

"How did this happen?" he demanded. "I ordered just the opposite!"

The Queen had saved the letter, and she showed it to the King. At once the King knew he had been tricked. He asked about the note, but the young man said he knew nothing of its contents.

"You shall not be let off so easily!" roared the King. "Anyone who is worthy of my daughter must fetch three golden hairs from the head of the Giant who lives nearby. If you bring these to me, then you shall keep my daughter as your bride."

The King was sure that this would be the end of the luck-child. For the Giant was so terrible that no one had ever escaped his clutches. But the young man merely smiled and set off.

On the way through town, he asked directions of the watchman at the gate. "In return, will you tell me why the fountain in our marketplace, from which wine used to flow, no longer gives even water?" said the watchman.

"You shall have the answer," said the luck-child, "upon my return."

At the next town, he asked directions of a second watchman. "In return," said the watchman, "can you tell me why a tree in our town, which once bore golden apples, now will not grow even leaves?"

"You shall have the answer," said the luck-child, "upon my return."

Finally he reached a ferryman, who took him across the river. "In return," said the ferryman, "will you tell me why I must always row back and forth and never be free?"

"You shall have the answer," said the youth, "upon my return."

At last he reached the Giant's huge castle. It was very gloomy. But the Giant was not at home. However, the Giant's grandmother was sitting in an armchair before the fireplace.

"I need three golden hairs from the head of the Giant," said the boy. "I must have them to keep my bride."

"You'll be lucky if you keep your head," said the old woman. "For my grandson is most fearful. If he sees you, things will go badly. However, I will try to help."

And with that, the old woman used her magic powers to change the young man into an ant. Then she put him in her apron pocket. "Just be quiet there," she said.

"One thing more," called the ant, "I must have the answers to three questions." And he repeated the questions for the old woman.

"I'll see what I can do," she said. "Just pay attention to what he says."

That evening the huge and disagreeable Giant stomped into the hall. "I smell the blood of a youth!" he bellowed at once.

"Oh, you are always smelling the blood of a youth," said his grandmother crossly. "Sit down and eat your supper."

After he had eaten, the Giant grew sleepy as usual. "Put your head in my lap and rest," the old woman said. And the Giant did.

As soon as the Giant began to snore, his grandmother plucked out one golden hair. "What are you doing?" he screamed.

"I just had a bad dream and pulled out a hair by mistake," his grandmother said. "In the dream, there was a fountain that used to pour wine. Now it is dried up. I wonder what that means."

"It means that a toad sits under the stone in the well," said the Giant. "If the toad is killed, the wine will flow again." And he fell asleep.

Soon the grandmother pulled out a second hair. "What are you doing?" he screamed.

"I had another dream," his grandmother said. "I dreamed there was a fruit tree that once bore golden apples. Now it does not even have leaves. What does that mean?"

"It means that a mouse is gnawing at the roots. If the mouse is killed, the apples will grow again," said the Giant. "And now leave my head alone, else I shall box you on the ear, grandmother or no."

As sometimes happens, the grandmother had no fear whatsoever of the Giant. So as soon as he fell asleep again, she plucked out a third hair.

Up jumped the Giant in a great fury, screaming and yelling. "I cannot help my bad dreams," said his grandmother, most calmly. "This time I dreamed of a ferryman who must go back and forth across the river and can never be free."

"The simpleton should put the oar in someone else's hand, and then he will be free," roared the Giant.

Then his grandmother left him in peace, and the Giant slept until daybreak. As soon as he had

gone, the old woman changed the ant back into a young man and gave him the three golden hairs.

The youth thanked her and went on his way. When the ferryman had taken him back across the river, the boy told him to give the oar to the next one he met who wished to cross.

He told the second watchman to chase the mouse that gnawed at the tree that used to give golden apples. The watchman gave him two barrels of gold in thanks.

He told the first watchman to chase the toad that was in the well so that wine would run out once again. The watchman gave him two more barrels of gold in thanks.

The Princess was very happy to see her husband when he returned. The King was not happy to see him at all. The young man gave the three golden hairs to the King. But the evil King was more impressed with the four barrels of gold.

"Tell me something," said the King. "Where did you get all this gold?"

"On the other side of the river," said the young man. "A ferryman will take you across and show you where there is lots more of it."

The King was as greedy as he was evil. And so at once he set off for the river. As soon as he stepped onto the ferryboat, the ferryman slapped the oar into his hand and sprang ashore.

The luck-child became the lord of the castle. He and the Princess lived happily ever after. As for the wicked and greedy King, he was doomed to row back and forth forever. And since no one has yet taken the oar from him, he must be ferrying still.

Edward and the Giant

Long, long ago, there was a beautiful Princess whom everyone loved. But one day, the Princess disappeared. Just like that, she was gone—and no one knew where. Her father the King was heart-broken. He promised a great reward to anyone who could find her. But no one did.

Not far from the palace lived a husband and wife and their three sons. The youngest son was not as handsome as his brothers, and his parents liked him less. They made him do all the work and let the older sons do whatever they pleased.

When the sons were grown, the eldest decided to seek his fortune in the world. His parents were sure that he would do well, and so they gave him a large part of their savings and new boots to wear.

After the eldest son had walked for a few miles, he became hungry. So he sat under a tree and started to eat the lunch his mother had given him. Just then a poor old man came by and asked for a bite of food. But the eldest son had never been taught to share anything. So he said, "I have scarcely enough food for myself, old man. Go and find your own." And the old man left.

The next day the eldest son again sat down to eat his lunch. A second old man asked for food. And, as before, the selfish son refused.

On the third day, the eldest son reached a great cave, which looked empty. He crept inside and fell asleep. In the middle of the night, he was awakened by a terrible roar. There in front of him stood a fierce, scowling Giant.

"This is my cave!" shouted the Giant. "What are you doing here?"

"Please don't hurt me," cried the eldest son. "I just wanted shelter for the night."

"Very well," said the Giant. "You may sleep the night. But in the morning you must do whatever I ask."

The eldest son agreed.

In the morning the Giant said, "I must leave for the day. While I am gone, I want you to sweep all the dust out of the cave. If it is not done when I return, it will be the worse for you."

The eldest son took the broom and began to sweep the cave. But the dust stuck to the floor, and he could not move it. So he sulked in a corner all day, wondering what the Giant would do.

He soon found out. The Giant returned and flew into a rage when he saw the dirty cave. Off

went the eldest son's head, and that was the end of him.

Some time later, the second son decided to seek his fortune in the world. His parents gave him a large part of their money and a new pair of boots.

As his brother had done, the second son sat down to eat his lunch on the first day, and the old man appeared, asking for food. But the second son had never been taught to share anything. So he refused the old man. And on the next day, he refused the other old man.

In time, the second brother also came to the cave of the Giant. He, too, was told to sweep the floor. But he could do no more than his older brother had done. So the second son also lost his head.

Now the youngest son, whose name was Edward, decided that he must go out into the world. His parents were glad to get rid of him, even though two of their sons had already gone. So they gave him a new pair of boots, and some food, and sent him away.

The young man followed the same road his brothers had taken, and after a while he sat down for lunch. In a few moments the old man appeared asking for food. Edward knew what it was to share. He said, "Of course, old man. I shall be glad of your company for lunch."

When he had eaten, the old man said, "If you are ever in trouble, call upon me. My name is Trull."

The next day the young man sat down under a tree to eat lunch. And the second old man appeared. Edward offered to share his food, and when they had finished, the old man said, "If you ever need help in even the smallest way, call upon me. My name is Brull."

On the third day of his travels, Edward came to the great cave of the Giant. He found it empty, and he went inside. There were many bones about, which made Edward shiver a bit, but he decided to sit down and wait for the Giant. For he was sure that a Giant lived there.

A few hours later, in strode the Giant. Politely, Edward asked if he might have shelter for the night.

"If you will agree to do whatever I ask in the morning," said the Giant. And the youth agreed.

The next morning the Giant told Edward to sweep the floor of the cave. Then the Giant left. Edward picked up the broom and began to sweep. But he could clean it no better than his brothers had done. Filled with despair at what he

was sure would be his fate, he sat upon the floor of the cave with his head in his hands. Then he remembered the first old man's words.

"Trull," he called, "I need your help."

Immediately the old man stood beside him. When Edward told him of his trouble, the old man said, "Broom, do your duty!" And the broom got up and danced about the cave. When it was through, there was not a speck of dust anywhere.

That evening, the Giant returned. When he saw the spotless cave, he said, "I cannot believe you did this alone. However, it is done, and so you may keep your head."

The next morning the Giant said, "You must take all the feathers out of my pillow and dry them in the sun. But if one feather is missing when I return, it will be the worse for you."

Edward spread the feathers from the Giant's pillow to dry in the sun. There were so many that they covered one entire hill. Before they could dry, a wind blew up, and the feathers began to dance in the air and blow away. At first Edward tried to catch them, but it was no use. Then he remembered the second old man's words.

"Brull, I need your help!" he called.

Hardly had he said the words than the second old man appeared before him. Edward explained his problem, and the old man shouted, "Birds, come and do your duty!"

Thousands of birds appeared in the sky. Each one found a feather and brought it back.

When the Giant returned that night, he counted all the feathers. "I cannot believe you did this alone," said the Giant. "But it is done as I wished, and you may keep your head."

The following morning, the Giant said, "If you complete one more task, I will set you free to go where you wish. And I will grant you three things besides. But if you fail, I will have your head!"

Then the Giant explained what he wanted the young man to do. "I have fifty oxen in my herd," he said. "You must guess which one I want to be killed. Then you must cook its heart before I return. If you kill the wrong one, you will lose your head!"

After the Giant had gone, Edward sat down to think. There was no way he could possibly guess which of the fifty oxen the Giant wanted to be killed. But then, once more, he thought of Trull and Brull.

"Trull and Brull," he called. "I need your help!"

In a few moments, he saw the two old men coming up the hill with an ox between them.

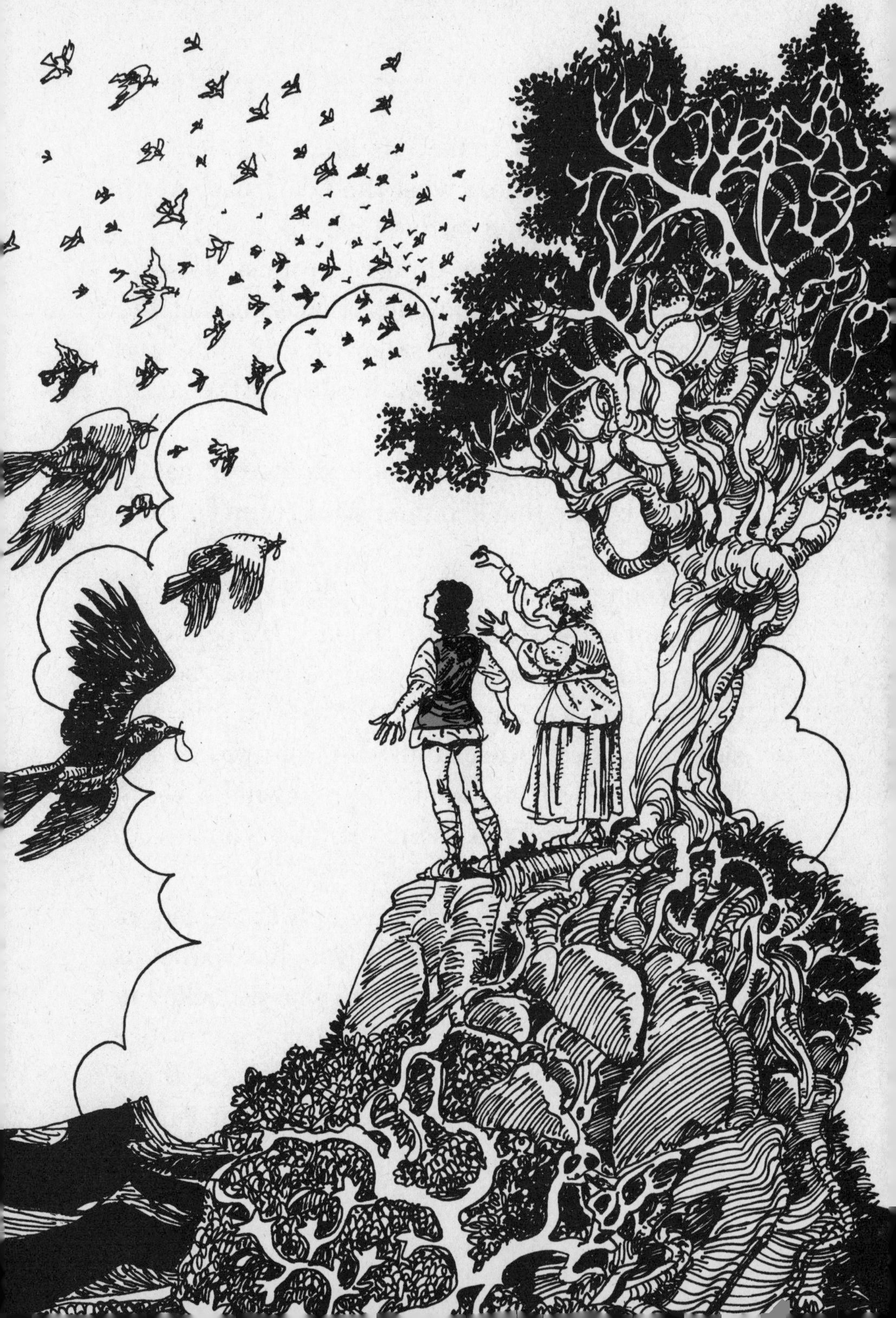

They killed it and cooked its heart. As they did so, Edward told them what the Giant had promised if he succeeded in this task.

"Here are the three things you must ask for," said Trull. "Ask for the chest that stands at the foot of the Giant's bed. Ask for what is under the cave. And ask for what is locked in the small chamber."

Edward thought these were strange things to request, but he thanked the two old men for their help.

No sooner had the old men disappeared than the Giant came striding up the hill. He could not believe his eyes when he saw the heart cooking on the stove. "I cannot believe you did this alone," he said. "But I must keep my word. You have succeeded, and tomorrow you will be free."

In the morning the Giant asked the young man what three things he wished.

"I will have the chest that stands at the foot of your bed," said Edward. "I will have what is under the cave. And I will have what is locked in the small chamber."

"I cannot believe that you chose these three things by yourself," said the Giant. "But I must keep my word. You will have the three things you request."

The chest that stood at the foot of the Giant's bed was full of precious rubies and diamonds. The young man would be rich for the rest of his life.

What was under the cave turned out to be a great sailing ship with magic oars and sails. Anywhere Edward wished to go, the ship would take him safely.

But the third request was the most astonishing of all. For what was locked in the small chamber turned out to be the beautiful missing Princess, who had been captured by the Giant.

"You must be the luckiest person ever born," said the Giant, as he watched Edward and the Princess walk down the hill toward the sea.

Edward pushed the heavy chest of precious stones onto the deck of the ship. Then he and the Princess stepped aboard.

"Take us to the home of the Princess," he commanded. At once, the ship sped off like the wind.

When the ship arrived at her kingdom, the Princess' father was filled with happiness. And for the next three days, there was great merrymaking and feasting and dancing everywhere.

Finally, when things calmed down a bit, the

King said to Edward, "How can I reward you for saving my beloved daughter?"

"I need no reward," replied Edward. "But if it is the Princess' wish, I would ask for her hand in marriage. I have fallen in love with her. I am not of royal blood, but I am now a wealthy man."

"If it is the Princess' wish," said the King, "I would be honored to have you in the royal family."

It was, indeed, the Princess' wish, for she had fallen in love, too. A great wedding was soon held, and the kind young man became a royal Prince.

And the Prince and the Princess lived happily for many years.

The Prince and the Giant

Long, long ago, there lived a King, his wife, and their son, the Prince. After the boy's mother died, the King met a richly dressed woman, whom he took as his second wife. The Prince grew to love his stepmother almost as much as he had loved his mother, and he liked to be by her side.

But one morning, the stepmother took the Prince aside, and said, "Today, you *must* go hunting with your father." When the Prince refused to go, the Queen scolded him, "No good will come of this," she said. Then she told the Prince to hide under her bed, and to stay there until she called him.

The Prince had been hiding under the bed for some time, when he heard what he thought must be an earthquake. The floor began to shake, and the palace walls began to rattle. Suddenly, he saw a huge giantess stride into the room and greet the Queen.

"Good morning, my sister," said the giantess. "Where is the Prince?"

"He is hunting with his father," replied the Queen. Then the giantess turned and left.

The next morning, the Queen again told the Prince that he must go hunting with the King. But again, the Prince refused. So the Queen made him hide under the table. This time, a second giantess appeared and greeted the Queen.

"Good morning, my sister," she said. "Where is the Prince?"

"Hunting," replied the Queen. "He is in the forest with the King."

The giantess looked under the bed, and said, "Are you sure the Prince is not hiding somewhere?"

"He is hunting," repeated the Queen. And so the giantess went away.

The next morning, the Queen took the Prince aside and begged him to join the King's hunting party. When the Prince refused, the Queen made him hide in the closet. This time, a third giantess greeted the Queen. She was even bigger than those who had come before.

"Good morning, my sister," roared the giantess. "Where is the Prince?"

"He is not here," replied the Queen. "He has gone hunting with his father."

But the giantess did not believe her. She looked under the bed and under the table. "Where is he hiding?" she roared.

But the Queen replied, "I have already told you that he is in the forest with the King."

"You are lying!" roared the giantess. "If he is close enough to hear my voice, he shall be half scorched and half withered. And he shall have neither rest nor peace until he finds me." And then she marched out of the palace.

As soon as the giantess was out of sight, the Queen ran to the closet. To her horror, the Prince was half scorched and half withered. "I begged you to go with your father," she cried, "but you would not listen. Now see what has happened."

Then she took the Prince into her room. "Hurry!" she cried. "Your father will be home soon!" She gave him a ball of string and three golden rings. "Drop the ball of string on the ground," she said, "and it will roll along until it leads you to the smallest giantess. Do not be afraid of her. Give her the smallest of these rings, as a present from me. This will make her happy, and she will offer to wrestle with you. Then, when you are tired, she will offer you a drink. She will not know it, but the drink will make you strong enough to conquer her. Then use the string to find the other two giantesses. But if a small dog lays its paws on you, you must come

home immediately, for my life will be in danger. Now, go, and remember that your stepmother loves you."

And so the Prince dropped the ball of string on the ground, and it rolled along until it came to the foot of a cliff. The first giantess looked down from the cliff and cried, "Aha! This is just what I wanted! The Prince shall go into the pot tonight!" Then she lowered a rope with a hook on the end, and hauled the Prince up to the top of the cliff.

The Prince was trembling with fear, but he handed the smallest of the three rings to the giantess. And it was just as his stepmother had said: the giantess was so pleased with the gift that she challenged him to wrestle with her.

Before long, the Prince was exhausted, and the giantess foolishly gave him a drink. With a few gulps of the drink, he became so strong that he easily overcame her.

Then the Prince dropped the ball of string to the ground, and it led him to the second giantess.

"Aha!" she cried. "The Prince shall go into the pot tonight!" But when the Prince gave her one of the rings, she was pleased, and she challenged him to wrestle with her. Again the Prince grew tired, and again, he was offered a drink. With a few gulps of the drink, he became so strong that he easily overcame her.

Then the Prince followed the ball of string to the third giantess. And when he had found her, he felt more peaceful and rested than he had ever thought possible. Then everything happened as it had before.

When the third giantess had been overcome, she said, "Not far from here, a beautiful girl stands at the edge of a sparkling lake. Take this magic ring, and give it to her."

So the Prince wandered along until he saw the girl by the lake. He gave her the ring, and they became friends. But when it was time for the girl to leave, she said, "You must not follow me home, for my father is a giant, and he will surely make a meal of you."

But the Prince would not leave her side, for he had fallen in love with her. When they neared her father's castle, the girl held the magic ring over the Prince's head. At once, he was turned into a bundle of wool. Then she carried the wool inside the castle, and placed it on her bed.

Just then, her father stomped into the room. His voice made the walls shake and the windows rattle. "I smell a man!" he roared, licking his lips

in hunger. He searched the room from bottom to top, but he did not find the Prince. Then he roared, "What is that lying on your bed?"

But his daughter replied, "It is only a bundle of wool." And so the giant went about his business.

The next day, when the giant left the castle, the girl held the magic ring over the bundle of wool. At once, the Prince took his own form again. Then the girl showed him all through the castle. She unlocked room after room, and after they had wandered through each room, she locked it again. But when they were finished, one key had not yet been used. Suddenly, the Prince noticed a heavy iron door he had not seen before.

"May I look in that room?" he asked.

"I dare not unlock it," said the girl. "It is forbidden." But the Prince kept after her until finally the door was unlocked and opened. Inside the room was a magnificent golden horse.

"Oh, I must ride him!" cried the Prince. But the girl turned pale with fear.

"No, never!" she whispered. "Father would be furious! No one is allowed to ride the golden horse."

"Oh, what harm would it do?" asked the Prince. "Just one short ride around the castle." Finally, the girl gave in, and the Prince mounted the golden horse. Then he saw a splendid sword with these words on the handle: *Whoever carries this sword and rides the golden horse shall find happiness.*

"Ah," sighed the Prince. "It is such a beautiful sword. Let me hold it for a moment."

The girl hesitated, and then said, "Since you are already on the golden horse, I suppose it could not hurt to hold the sword as well. But if you do, then you must also carry these." And she handed him a small stone, a wooden stick, and a dried-up twig that had been next to the sword.

"Of what use are these old things?" asked the Prince, taking the stone, the stick, and the twig.

"My father says they are more valuable than the horse and the sword," explained the girl. "When the twig is thrown to the ground, it instantly becomes a thick forest. And when someone strikes the stick against the stone, giant hailstones instantly bring death to his enemies. Now, if you must, ride once around the castle, and return to this room before my father comes home."

The Prince rode once around the castle on the beautiful golden horse. And a small dog ran along behind him. Suddenly the dog jumped up, and put its paws on the Prince's knee. The Prince

remembered his stepmother's words: "If a small dog lays its paws on you, you must come home immediately, for my life will be in danger." So, instead of riding the golden horse back to the room with the iron door, the Prince galloped off across the fields.

When the giant returned, he found the heavy iron door open, the room empty, and his daughter in tears. The girl was terrified, and she told her father everything that had happened. With a mighty roar, the giant strode out of the castle and across the fields. And each huge stride brought him closer and closer to the Prince.

As soon as the Prince saw the giant, he threw the twig to the ground. At once, a thick forest grew up in front of the giant. It was so dense that the giant could not pass. But the giant took out a huge axe, and chopped a path through the trees.

Soon the giant was almost close enough to reach out and seize the tail of the golden horse. But the Prince struck the stick against the stone, and huge hailstones began to fall on the giant. They were as large as boulders and they instantly killed him.

The Prince rode on, and arrived at his stepmother's palace just in time. The King had returned from the hunt, and had accused the

Queen of killing her stepson. And just as the servants were about to hang the Queen, the Prince galloped up. He drew the sword, and cut the rope in two.

The King was overjoyed to see his son alive and well. And as the Prince told of his adventures, tears of joy came to the King's eyes.

Suddenly the Prince mounted the golden horse again, and rode away. When he returned, he had with him the giant's daughter.

They were married the next day, and everyone said there was never a more beautiful bride or a more deserving groom. And of course, they lived happily for many, many years.